This final book is the culmination of over two years work.

In 2020 I started out on an incredible

of an idea.

" Who wants to write a collaborative p

Several of you jumped at the opportunit ... it began. I wrote a verse, one person wrote the next and on and on it went. The only stipulation was they had to use at least one word from the last line of the previous verse.

265 people of all ages, from all over the world have added a verse. Some of them have written 2 verses, others 3.

It was my very first collaboration. I have lost count on how many collaborations I have been involved in since then. Every one has been a joy.

There are people in Joined Up Writing, who have now died, others I no longer get on with, some of the poets I don't even know. Just a name on a page. There are parents and children, husbands and wives, and brothers. Also several relatives of mine. There are people who I would have liked to have taken part, but for whatever reason didn't. There are a quite few who had never written anything before.

I thank you all.

Below are all the names: in order of writing.

Such names, such writers.

Such a pleasure to curate and edit this series of books.

1 Fin Hall

2 Violet Wilde

3 Hannah Nicholson

4 Sid Ozalid

5 Fiona-Jane Brown

6 Bruce Alexander Davidson

7 Angela Joss

8 Kimberly Petrie

9 Jo Gilbert

10 Ellen Bain

11 Colin Clyne

12 Annie Begg

13 Laurence Petre Alan

14 John Bolland

15 Arizona Mercedes Brodie

16 Zander Ran

17 Birgit Itsen

18 Alison Chandler

19 Orla Kelly

20 Kirsty Franklin

21 Chris Crichton

22 Rudy Punchard

23  Jamie McCormick

24 Liam Barr

25  Stephen Hall

26 Aurora Rory Buccheri

27 Ali MacKenzie

28  Andy Bisset

29  Janine Rae

30  Teresa Fraser

31 Andy Talbot

32 Pam Benjamin

33  Sue Beesley

34 Wendy Ivers

35  Kris McCorquodale

36  Alex Morrison

37 Duncan McKenzie

38 Stewart Alexander Noble

39 Alan Tweedy Digweed

40  Bert Timmermans

41  Michelle Donna-Marie E Rivers

42 Davy Hepburn

43 Craig Atkinson

44 Kaitlyn Robertson

45 Simon Maryan

46  Kevin Coronel

47 Ron Bird

48 Peter Wood

49 James Karpowicz

50 Geoff Woodger

51 Dana Lirosi

52 Dave Bremner

53 Ian Smith

54 Jamie McMillan

55 Alma Morrison

56 Gaye Anthony

567 Alex Winsley

58 Ian Williams

59 Dave Lumsden

60 Gerry Kennedy

61 Robert Plunkett

62 Andy Brown

63 Scott Graham

64 Claire Sweeney

65 Flavious Grindean

66 Bryan Morrison

67 Rachel Thomson

68 Batt Breathnach

69 Neil Dalrymple

70 Diana Peers

71 Vix Bloomfield

72 Chris Gatensby

73 Ellen Streger

74 Douglas McDonald

75 Aron Smith

76 Joan Hall

77 Angustine Sutherland

78 Shan Gordon

79 Stella Winters

80 Sally Givertz

81 Lisa Elrick

82 Mark Elrick

83 Jim McKean

84 Beth Hartley

85 Charlie Scott

86 Shirley Cruikshank

87 Holly Jackson

88 Anathema McKenna

89 Heather Milne

90 Wilma Dean-Prasad

91 Heather Claughan

92 Christine Fowler

93 Mandy Maxwell

94 Cat Perry

95  Brian Plunket

96  Scott Coe

97  Jasmine Brae Triance

98  Sarah Anne Smith

99 Chris Begg

100  Arya Rae

101  Bryan Ira Franco

102 Hil Hoover

103  Noel Lena Marie

104 Kimberly Johnson ( Special K )

105 Dana Malone

106  Jo Collins

107  Dane Ince

108  Skylar J Wynter

109  Erin Gannon

110  Kayla Sue Bruyn

112  Francesca Kirkpatrick

113  Mel Bradley

114  Jacqueline Morey-Grace

115  Isobel White

115  Kate Jenkinson

116 Graham McPherson

117  Kelly Van Nelson

118  Greg Slade

119  Francis Golm

120  Bob Kenyon

121  Caroline in Bristol

122  Tanya Southey

123  Maire Stephen

124  Mark Symonds

125  Leslie Constable

126  Hazel Mehmet

127  Caroline Low

128  Jon Wesick

129  Cynthia Winfield

130  Andy N

141  Amanda Steel

142  Rick Spisek

143  Cathi Rae

144  John Guzlowski

145  Lisa Johnson

146  Bob Whelan

147  Michael Sindler

148  Dig Wayne

149  Kelly Buchan

150  Pankhuri Sinha

151  John F McMullen

152  Shruti Shukla

153  Rhoda Thomas

154  Katie Thomson

155  Noah Levin

156  Rhian Brooke

157  Catherine Skalda

158  Lynn Lane

159  Kemlyn Tan Bappe

160  Christine Hall

161  Tricia de Jesus-Gutierrez

162  Vi Dragonlady

163  Rebecca Elazaar

164  Emma Louise Ormond

165  David Lewis

166  Anna Lindsay

166  Samantha Mansi

168  Jo Collins

169  Eden Selvedge

170  Christine Dickinson

171  Star Anderson

172  Abdoula Mansour

173  Kayan Van Nelson

174  Nathalie Sallegren

175  Halima Malek

176  Richard Harries

177 Juanita Rea

178 Erika A Tilley

179 Chris Begg

180 Rachel Carlton

181 Beci Guy

182 Marissa Prada

183 Margaret O' Reagan

184 Henry L Jones

185 Therese Craine Bertsch

186 Nina Adel

187 David Rodriguez

188 Megan Chapman

189 David Leo Sirios

190 Martina McGowan

191 Deborah Ramos

192 Andrew Martin

193 Sylvia Ang Lay Kheng

194 Andrew Martin

195 Anna Catrice

196 Jiawen Lin

197 Annalisa Jackson

198 Skylar Yap

199 Meher Pestonji

200 Janet Kuypers

201 Gary Huskisson

202 Kev Bamboo

203 Tim Evans

204 Tina J Cox

205 Justine Aborgine

206 Anna Somerset

207 Rebecca Lowe

208 Deepkirian Garlapadu

209 Zaheera Badat

210 Xavier Panades Blas

211 Xanthi Hondrou-Hill

212 Caroline Walling

213 Claire McWilliams

214 Timothy Evans

215 Ian Prezanowski

216 Phil Knight

217 Antionette Vella Payne

218 Paul R Kohn

219 Elijah Kohn

220 Jadon Kohn

221 Doc Janning

222 Ann Atkins

223 Kizzy Wade

224 Pete Blunden

225  Anneka Niro

226  Daniel Kaye

227  Alan Wong

228  Mantis Diego Tabogan

229 Yvonne Ugarte

230  Sophia Behal

231 Giovanna McKenna

232  Ceitidh Chaimbeul *

233  Randy Horton

234 Seb Lastre *

235  L âme aux Rimes *

236  Guillaume, Le Bricoleur d'ìdées *

237 Amy Hoskins

238   Victoria Jeu

239  Brendon Clark

240  Jaycee Workman

241  Red Medusa

242  Squigs

243  Laura Grevel

244  Mandy Mc Donald

245  Rawls James

246  Blair Centre

247 Catriona Noble

248  Brian Burchette

249 Danielle Boyles

250 Lisa Louise Lovebucket

251 Leas Cullen

252 Sonia Bailey

253 Emma Sloan

254 Lia Nogueira

255 Mahal Kuh

256 Michael Gerard Collins

257 Dominic Williams

258 Kusum Choppra

259 Lindsey Oliver

260 Martina Gallegos

261 Nabellea Ahmed

262 Owuso Nyamo Frederick

263 Osebre Adeline Ann

264 Linda Jaxson

265 Dany Morgan

265 Grace Evans

*Translations at the end of the book.

Other books by Author.

Joined Up Writing: 100 Voices, 2020

Joined Up Writing: The Second Installment 2021

Once Upon A Time There Was, Now There Isn't: 2021

Solidarity: 2022

Published by Like A Blot From The Blue 2022.

2.104
The pride I fee
Unlike any other feeling.Warms me, enthrals me,
From last May until now
Words that awed, words that wowed.
Sharing words, caring words.
Words from strangers.  Words from friends.
Thank you for the words.
Joining words from the beginning, to the very, very end.
Fin Hall

## Joined Up Writing:  Three Fall

3.01.
And in the beginning
A new light shone from your eyes
Naked in the bright morning
Joining words to a new realm of possibilities
And singing my shining  dreams
From the start of the journey
Down the corridors of history
To the very very end.    Tim Evans

3.02
The very, very end...
Well, that's around the bend
The road is straight
Then, you choose your fate I would turn right
It's pretty much, in sight
But if you go the other way
You will be driving all day.  Tina J Cox

3.03
I will rumble up, in a jaunty little pickup
without preparing a pickup line,
You'd be right there bent over picking up crabapples
and I'd get a nice view of your behind. Justine Aborogine

3.04
The view from the tower is strangely subdued.
 Pubs all shut.
 Village green silent.
 But alive in my memories with chaotic maypole dancing,
Dangerous old school coconut shies

And the bizarrely exciting pick an-egg-stall.
When you picked the one that wasn't a shell your heart soared,
 But mine never arrived back whole.  Anna Somerset

3.05
Not whole, but fragmented,
the memories come - shards of broken glass that refuse
to piece together - At night,
he will sit and cry the battlefield
on sweated sheets, cry like a baby,
And nothing I can say
will bring him round - the sound
of gunfire ricochets the trees,
And in the darkness jagged shapes appear -
And all I can do, is hold him close and pray.  Rebecca Lowe

3.06
Pray to the god of fish contemplation
Bow to the flame of inspiration
Time to kneel for your deep clean preparation
Hold him close for each incarnation
Rich man breading maintains mutation
Never brought up in polite conversation
Silver spoon body swerves allegation
Lack of education can cause dehydration
When you pray to the god of…
Fish contemplation.  Sid Ozalid.

3.07
fish contemplation can spontaneously occur at the lakeside…
perhaps because he becomes suddenly aware that his life
has almost unfolded.
he is curious
about his future…
where he might be going.
he may perhaps be an animal…
always feeling he has been  in over his head
he wonders…
would he come back as a water dweller,
perpetually floating pretending to dream?
then just as suddenly  he is awakened to the reality of his
now…
in a park, on the shore ofLake Michigan
where children run in time with the rhythms of a
fountain…Bob Whelan

3.08
The world revolves in the eternal rhythm of love and affection.
And I sit wondering
I didn't finish explaining
Life is for, living, hoping ,loving,
A pulsatile being,
there is no black and white,
It's not a straight line,
A single wave envelopes us,
In a rhythmic lore,
Now, after,  death ,forever ,life goes on more and more,
Luring the soul for abundant connections,
Some corrections and additions,
Beautiful surrections..
The world revolves in the eternal rhythm of love and affection.
Deepukiran Garlapadu.

3.09
Love waxes and wanes to pummel and salve, a vacillating soul
savagery
Plucking stitches from wedding bonnets
Adding the same to coffin cloth
An elegant undulation of birthing new life
And halting heartbeats
In guises of gold and gargoyle true love conquers all... Zaheera
Badat

3.10
Love without kindness brings harmony,

erects monuments of eternal love,

completes promises forgotten in time,

leaving space for darkness to arise. Xavier Panades Blas

3.11
Leaving space for darkness to arrive...
Embrace the depths of oaths,
the passion of heroes,
respect the darkness of the villain inside.  Xanthi Hondrou-Hill

3.12
Respect the invisible that creates shadows within light.
A chaos primary, universal centre.
There is no ground without sky,
 no birth without death,
 no solid space without yielding.
Respect the sand it kicks up

The line it draws.
Respect the fusion of forces that divide you,
each is a seed for the other.   Caroline Walling.


3.13
Each one full of the ancestral pulp of past.
Ancient accumulation.
Forever growing.
Cultivated, nurtured,
loved, let go.
To inform our present
To excite our days
To ensure our future.  Clare McWilliams.


3.14
I lie here staring at a future
Announcing itself in the ring of a phone wondering
Who the hell could…
The morning goes about its business Bringing birth and death
to day (having no stake in the game)
Our bodies lie in the ashes of our Fucking  its morality
Never coming into play, we tell each Other fables of
Being in the moment, all that bullshit About nothing
Being guaranteed, we take  shelter in a Temple of our own
design not giving a
Fuck about "neither here nor there"
Our house of cards secure enough,
Out in the air a child's  plaintive cry,
And the feet of morning moving the day along.
Timothy Evans


3.15
As time marches guided by the smile of the sun
Content, I bask in the glory of its splendour
As  fading shadows chase the rising smile
The silent shout of the glacial peak unveiled
Still against the howl of the whispering wind    Ian Prezanowski


3.16
The whispering wind inspired me
with thoughts romantic and culinary
so, to create a recipe for love
I took some stars from the sky above
I then added a pinch of bliss,
for good measure, a tender kiss
to this, the innocence of a prom corsage
plus, the contentment of a great massage.
What else to add? This can't be wrong,
the gentle breath of a baby, just born.

Of course, it needs a master's art,
a Rembrandt painting that moves my heart.
Combine the feeling of a warm summer rain
with a saxophone solo by Coltrane.
Mix in the care of a dear friend,
a sprinkle of rosebuds to the blend.
For loyalty, a golden ring.
I did not want to miss a thing!
To make perfect my cuisine
the fragrance of a meadow, lush and green.
I followed the recipe, but
I had this feeling in my gut
though still a romantic,
I can see that this was not the dish for me.  Joan Hall.

3.17
For revenge is a dish best served hot.
Cold vengeance is as tasteless as week old bread.
It is the heat that brings out the flavours.
Fresh from the oven the smell fires the senses,
So strong you could almost feed on the scent
But that is just the prelude, the instant
Of anticipation that almost lasts an eternity.
However the proof of the pudding
Is in the eating, or so they say.  Phil Knight

3.18
Or so they say
Flavor an acquired taste
Like muffins born in a barn
Heat's resurrection
Breath of life
Her body swells from
One grain to sustenance
With tiny bits of sweetness
To carry us through.   Antionette Vella Payne

3.19
To carry us through
we held our bodies like temples

holy ground only we know
how to survive the test

of time and see beauty
in scars becoming

sacred text
script only we know

how to read the stories
behind the bleeding.  Sarah Bellum-Mental

3.20
My heart is bleeding out…
As forked lies stab it over and over
with the truth's they led me to believe;
the truth that they would always be there,
that I could call on them in my time of need,
that I am family and they would stay…
My heart is bleeding out…
But that's its job isn't it?
Its echo reverberates in my head.
Thump… Thump… Thump…
The same sound the slamming door made
when they turned their back and left
right when I needed them the most;
Someone… Anyone… "Thump…" Nothing…
Its echo reverberates in my head;
silence, loneliness, the sound of my new normal.
I miss them more than they could ever know.
But love does not die easily, and mine is unconditional.
And yet that is so very misunderstood by others
who can only love with conditions, with control.
Yet even in the missing, in the loneliness,
in the pain and breaking of my bleeding heart,
I miss them more than they could ever know.
And I remain loyal should they ever need me.
There is strength in softness, softness in strength.
And despite everything, I am strong.
I needed to lose everything to realise
that I am everything I need and more.

That unconditional love just is, without
expectations, conditions, reciprocation.
There is strength in softness, softness in strength.
Anger and revenge always fall away to unconditional love.
Paul R Kohn

3.21
Revenge is what I hate.
When I get them with a prank,
they always get me back
but I'm never able to get them back.
Who cares??? I DO!!!
Because it can hurt your best mate.
Someone could push you into a puddle and you get all wet.
Then when you're not thinking, you push them back in
and the puddle turns red because their nose has bled.
You don't want that happening to you, do you?
If you don't, you should just leave the them be.
Otherwise the pranks could keep on going forever.
You see revenge is kind of like life;
a prank is played and revenge is born.
Pranks upon pranks are used and then
one person decides to stop.
Revenge dies and friendship lives on.   Elijah Kohn

3.22
'Will this friendship end?'
I think, lying next to them.
I don't want it to.
They are important
to me, someone I value.
My friend through it all.  Jadon Kohn

3.23
Through all the Multiverse time seeks
        ever for its Self
        for its essence and its being
        for its beginning and its end
        ever wondering
        ever questioning
            Does it exist?   Doc Janning

3.24
Does it exist,
or is it a figment of my imagination?
A ghostly apparition here to haunt me.
If I close my eyes tight will it go away?
Perhaps everything we believe is illusory
and we are all characters in someone else's dream.    Ann
Atkins

3.25
We all dream as if we're a character with prewritten plot,
We hope for creative control but also a crew we can blame if
everything goes wrong,
We're all characters in a film with the most obvious ending,
But I guess the question is who do we pitch it too,
Or who will watch the duration,
And who will leave at the interval?  Kizzy Wade

3.26
And who will leave in this hour of need
When this needless necessity
And negotiation
Will lead to nonplussed negotiations
Of desperation?
Who is left when despair rules over
And disparity
Separates
From solidarity
And we are all left alone?
Who will come to our aid,
Who will be left to fight for rights
Who will leave us staggering
And why do we stand?
What becomes of life?
If all we are, were and will be is here,
What can we be proud of?
A thumbprint in immortal sands,
And all we have is laid bare to be washed away
By wind and storms.
Measures of immediate certainty undone
By grinding cosmic dogmas.
What can we do but rage against universal truth?
Pete Blunden

3.27
Mere truths at their core
Open wounds and gaping sores
Which hurt more.  Anneka Niro

3.28
It hurt more the pain
No one understood,
She wishes it would rain.  Samantha Mansi

3.29
She wished it could rain,
Hoping the heavens would cleanse her sins
With a calming shower
That would plant gentle kisses upon her skin.
May the raindrops
Compose their lullabies as they greet the earth,
Awaken her soul with the breath of life
And grant nature the promise of rebirth.  Daniel Kay

3.30
She smiled at nature.
Nature arranged an awesome place for her.
She is very blessed.  Alan Wong

3.31
The sky is full of scrawled songs
Peering down on the readers
Busying themselves with tasks and runs
To and from their daily destinations. So few
Look up, stick their necks up
And out to the horizon.
Best kept secrets have the most simple
Laughably innocent cloaks to don. Mantis Diego Toboggan

3.32
stripped bare to innocent original form
unswaddled from many layered maxims
tentative tenets formed from direct spark
released untamed still wet unblemished
soon scarred, carved, bent and sullied
broken back into well-worn pallid pattern
ready now the red pencil and eraser
with each revision tales become clearer.  Michael Sindler

3.33
With each new dawn,
fragments of hope appear,
 tiny sparks of silver that permeate the darkest corners of the
Pandora's Box of horror
 newly released into our world.   Yvonne Ugarte

3.34

LOVE needs to be released newly
into our world again and again,
forever.
HATE needs to disappear silently
into the dark, again and again,
forever.
FRIENDSHIP needs to exist fully
between you and me, again and again,
forever
HUMANITY needs to be one completely
all over the world, again and again,
forever.  Sophia Behal


3.35

Global world mind thoughts race,
eyes wide, world pandemic risk
Infection Terror Being.  Sweat
down side of temple.  Escalate,
pulse rate.  Can't sleep.  Blood
shot sight says shut off the news.
Temple pulse throb.  Breathing
caught in back of throat.
Close eyes – calm.  Old days
flash.  Where are you all?  No!
Walk down empty road and
cracked pavement will trip your
genuine 100% full imitation pimp
strut.  Redefine abject past reality
and say the golden days were
there.  Sucker punch your
memories with the fist of a liar.
Another cup of coffee and another
day.  World on edge.  Sip slow.
There's sunshine there.  Put cheek
to window and feel warmth.
Absorb now.  Be now.  Chaos
swirls on horizon.  Pressure front
of AP news brings tidings, but not
today.  Switch dial, turn on the
radio and listen to Satchmo play.
He knows.  Smile now, happiness
awash self with tear in eye.  Noah Levin

3.36

Close one eye, and then another.

Look for fireworks.

Feel their flashing burn

spark infernos in your belly.

Watch the shifting blaze

of colour scorch and char your heart.   Giovanni MacKenna

3.37

Dark is to light, as light is of dark.
Flung so far together,
Driven so hard to depart.
Soft and light, hard and heavy-
The fire it sparks.
The smoke rises to signal
The changing of the guard.
The flicker at the fade is much the same as it is at the start.
Black and red and dry as a sky,
Frozen still in the gaze
Of such long dead stars.
Is it any wonder- the longing?
We are born to be burning inside.
Born into taking the pain into our arms…
Is living any more than only burning just right?   Greg Slade.

3.38

Watching his brown kindling flesh burning, basted with
screams
echoing through smoke
While hearing layers pop like crackling awaiting hungry
mouths to feed the youth
Fires cooking out the memories of muscle which once moved
with grace now bound by twisted fear
Sacred fumes rise as the last breaths of life exhale as one long
scream
But no one hears the ghost leaving and has no tears to
extinguish the hell
The hung evil awaits redemption to see light in the glow of
warmth as hands reach
Palms applaud and mouths cheer the Devil is dead as they hope
this sacrifice will help them sleep at night.   Henry L Jones

3.39 *
Nuair a thig dorchadas an oidhche tharta,
cuiridh e comhdanach de sàmhachais orra
is an comhradh air a mhùchadh.
An àire air na thachair fo ghrèim-bàis balbhachd.
Cha robh na crìdhean aca facal a radh
is ainneamh a bhruidhinn iad. Ceitidh. Chaimbeul


3.40
They seldom spoke, they seldom wrote, they seldom raised a
fuss,
but resurgence is always possible. Passion may always surge.
Once tepid waters can regain a roiling boil,
and the timid may find redemption through new acts of
heroism.
The beaten brow rises once again to send a new warning.
Randy Horton


3.41 *
Une fois de plus à l'aube,
Une lueur d'espoir se montre !
C'est bien d'avoir peur, c'est ok d'avoir peur. la question est...
 Saurons-nous saisir ou fuirons-nous des opportunités
inconnues ? Seb Lastre


3.42 *
Fuirons-nous le bonheur prêté par notre innocence,
Ne restons pas aveugles au prix de l'ignorance,
Notre colère portée comme une arme, l'espoir aiguise nos
lames,
Nous battant pour le futur, et la valeur de nos âmes. Beci Guy


3.43 *
Même sous le feu du Napalm, l'âme des braves perdure
Quand des jugements infâmes, comme tant de balles perdues
Envoient le message que tout est bon pour défendre son camp
Si c'est par amour est-il vraiment sage d'aimer jusqu'au sang?
L'âme aux Rimes


3.44 *
Il est l'heure de l'âge des sages,
L'heure de comprendre que nous ne sommes que de passage,
Sortir du temps pour revenir à l'instant
Oublier nos barrières pour la danse et le chant
Nous sommes des êtres de lumière
Faits pour briller plus chaleureusement qu'un éclair
Sentir sa poitrine, son ventre et son front
Tu la sens cette énergie des émotions ?
Guillaume, Le Bricoleur d'idées

3.35

No-el, It doesn't feel like Christmas to me
I don't want it to be Christmas at all
Just can't bear all this Yuletide cheer
Reduced as it is by the Omicron stall
The turkey is getting smaller, the present piles reduced
As another loved one is holidaying in heaven or in hell
It's meant to celebrate a birth so joyous, a miracle to behold
So why do the Queen's speech and Strictly leave me so cold
I comfort myself by mimicking the overspending and the gluttony
As bank accounts decrease and waistbands increase exponentially
This Cinderella doesn't want to go to the ball, in fact
I don't want it to be Christmas at all.   Caroline Low


3.36

Christmas is always mixed: drink up, It's the holidays,
 We didn't want to spoil you by getting you what you wanted,
Christmas baking, making secret plans for Christmas morning,
betrayal and losses, to now:
sitting outside admiring Cardinals, Chickadees, Finches:
in the garden we have made with loving hands.  Amy Hoskins


3.37

With living hands
We cultivate and modelling make our stand, we mould in clay
each sacred day.
These living hands reach out to touch
The hearts out there that means so much
These living hands can sculpt from sand
Eternal verities beyond the strand,
across the stars and galaxy
And might place upon your lip
This gentle kiss    Rick Spisek


3.38

Your place to gently kiss goodbye
Why and wherefore you cannot tell
Seal your lips, never speak
Upon this heart
Words warning quell.  Victoria Jeu

3.39

Quell your warning words,
Hold your fire inside,
For all the times you tried
To hide
You were seen, by me.
For all you have been,
Who you were, you are, for
Who you could be.
Hold fast the hate,
Hold fast your fears
Release your tears and I will
Catch them all.
Return to me.
Return to me in hope, in love.  Brendon Clark

3.40

I raise my pen in love, in hope
and quite a bit of fear;
I pace, I  sigh, then pace some more,
willing genius to appear.
With furrowed brow and focused gaze
I raise the quill, intent.
Can great acclaim be far behind
When you read my lament?
I see it all, head back, eyes closed
snuggled in my chair.
What shall I wear to sign my books?
Of course, I have amazing flair...
 Now to my dismay it seems
I dwelt too long in mind
anticipating my new life
has taken all my time
Sadly no great things were writ,
no ideals newly espoused
This literary lioness,
Revealed as a sad mouse!   Jaymee Workman

3.41

Majestic lion
is revealed as a sad mouse,
when life permits truth. Red Medusa

3.42

Death permits deceit.
Autumn moons rise
Beyond vermillion horizons.
Soldiers mark unmarked graves
In chalk. Filling holes

With carbine sent messages
Families will never read.
Gifting unwanted freedom
To unknown souls without
Without permission.
Life permits truth as
Truth permits lies.  Lynn Lane


3.43
it is in the dilation of a pupil which permits
a rough draft of sunset, to be trapped
in the grasp of an eyelid
it is an ocean dying upon a palm
in the shape of a tear, running still
where your fingertips once were
it is a promise fastened against
the inconstant dawn, as further
furnaces sphered into alignment
a suffocating horizon now persists in
a parade of missteps, feet winded
with hands reaching a degrading orbit
it is a feather, where a pillow should be
a space between our arms
a cocoon tears and your lips part
it is just breath into lead
a pencil into cassette
where a loudness exists
 before a whisper. Squigs


3.44
Loudness and whispers clash
In my head
Strident voices
Expressing anger and hate
And discord
Combating the soothing whispers of love
Peace and joy
Which will win?
For my sanity I hope the quiet one.  Richard Harries


3.45

The quiet garden is what I'll seek

In these nights of need

In the peril of these days

That snarl like starving dogs

Hunting for fresh meat.  Laura Grevel

3.46

Hunting for peace,

Tranquility

Places of refuge

Resting place

From war and chaos

Space to breathe  Andy Bisset

3.47
Keep wondering if space is
really what you need,
if the ratio of declared need – a new
vacuum, fulfilment, a beer, to see your
best friends, some buttermilk for the biscuit
recipe, a better vehicle - to true
human need is accurate,
if the list of six things you couldn't
live without ((seven if you break the rules
of the game) is reasonable,
appealing, inoffensive, clever;
if the use of two tablespoons of lemon
juice in milk, or long-term solitude,
are comparable, in the world, to a lack.  Nina Adel

3.48
There's no lack of brambles here
along our allotment's back border, a stockade of them,
fretful in November, still a few little tart fruits.
Their long canes wind in amongst the rosebay willow-herb,
pink cathedral spires loud with bees and the wasps
who have nested in the old compost heap.
No lack of brambles, either, a friend tells us,
returning tanned and brimming with stories
from the Galapagos, the fairytale islands.
They're everywhere, the *moras*,
querulous, snagging, strangling,
 The climate is perfect for them
and everything that eats them
carries their seed away.

We brought them there, of course,
a mere half-century ago,
as we've brought so many pestifers –
dogs, cats, rats, knotweed, brambles –
to so many lands we thought of as ours
to tailor to our needs and our caprices,
never content with the cornucopias of fruits
and trees and creatures they offered us so freely.
We always have to meddle. So the *moras* invade,
thick-woven as the thorn-jungle cast
around the Sleeping Beauty's tower.
Only this jungle won't disappear
at the touch of a good fairy's wand.
Beware humans when they come bearing gifts.
Mandy McDonald

3.49
beware of humans bearing gifts -
wine when you've stopped drinking, a book
when you've had enough of thinking, cheeses
that can end up stinking your fridge out,
try and avoid rifts
drink grape juice whilst they down the wine
say you'll enjoy reading the thing when you next have time
get them to sniff the cheese
before they dine.  Rhoda Thomas

3.50
A memory flashed of what occurred before
It consumed her into an inward panic
I reached for her as she headed for the  door
As she suddenly got oddly sad, and manic.  Rawle James

3.51
As she suddenly got oddly sad, and manic
she pushed her way through the iron gate
to escape this manic state.
She did not wait to discern,
"Is this the pathway to my home?"
Half crazed and running down familiar streets she did not meet
a single soul
Quite full of dread and very cold
she whispered , "Am I dead?"
Had she been there before?
Is it what it seemed or just a dream?
No, she'd been there many times
A stranger to myself I did not see the terrors that invaded her,
had just invaded me
Thérèse Craine Bertsch

3.52
Stranger was a word I thought
I should never utter or think he should become,
nor he did of I; we are
standing on the cliff
of indecision, wondering
where to walk next on our sojourner's
journey. The dark moody
clouds and the smells of
the green moor permeating
our lungs and souls, causing us
to breathe a bit more importantly.
I had thought of the roads to nowhere,
that indeed got us somewhere. We
look at each other, and
think why bother,
the cool rain bringing us
back to a present that
suddenly seemed like
crossroads to a future only we could decide on.
Katie Thompson

3.52
This is my future
games and fun,
but also
sad and glad.
Sooner or later
the sun will rise and
the owls will hoot.
We will play,
go back to school,
and have a hoot-tastic time. Rebecca Elazar

3.53
Time's force is tough and rough to put to rout;
it incessantly marches through life's plains
and, although Time is always running out
and away, it retreats not. The day wanes,
and comes again, but different it is
upon each rotation and new return
and every night approaches, passes
by, and for those former nights we then yearn.
Yet, do not give in to all Life's worries;
try to carve out your own space of sweet bliss.
Although it seems that Old Time does hurry,
its ancient magic cannot prevent this:

you months and years are yours alone to use;
so, fill them with love and fun, if you choose.  Blair Center

3.54
Use fun to decipher your success in life.
Take time to collect your thoughts
and reflect on the meanings
of all the seemingly simple things
that bring you joy and happiness.
Don't second guess this.
Rediscover your passion and skills!
We have one life to live
make sure it's your dreams
you manifest, your life's purpose you fulfil.  Kate Jenkinson.

3.55
Manifest with vision boards, manifest with prayers
Regardless of religion, self-doubt and Naysayers
Believe in all you wish for, trust your inner voice
It is the guiding Force in you, revealing your true choice.
Catriona Noble

3.56
Revealing dreams. At that moment I scream in a subconscious
realm.
At the helm of great aspiration.
Seeking a great destination.
Hoping that the proclamation.
Can reveal a destination and a path.  Brian Burchette

3.57
On a particularly dreich winters night, a small man stood
staring, on a  path
The blue winds bit and chewed at his flesh as he searched for
his long gone marbles. Unfortunately for him, they had fled
with the better weather.
Fraserburgh has a lot to answer for. Husks of humans roam the
grotty streets, their insides are as hollow as the town itself. The
only plaza is a designated meeting point, where stands a rusting
statue of a long forgotten figure. The statue's gaze takes in all
of the abhorrent goings on, with nicotine-yellow street lights
regretfully illuminating the despair.
The small man was oblivious to the heroin addicts who were
robbing the adjacent corner shop. Not a grimace graced his
gnarling face as the howls of an enraged shop keeper thundered
from the shop.
He just stood. Feet glued to the pavement by years of
unfathomable depression and loneliness. A heaviness too thick
to consider. He just stood.

The gang of men spewed from the corner shop. Confusion and anger echoed round the the square as the small man just stood staring. There was no reaction from him in the slightest as they roared past, pockets full of sweets, fags and the pathetic contents of the shopkeeper's till. His face remained expressionless as he was knocked to the ground by the last of the assailants. Neither did it alter when his head met the pavement with the same tone as a rotten coconut.

The only thing that changed for the small man as he lay staring on the street corner, was the all encompassing question now swallowing up his head:

"What kind of fated destiny is this?"   Kelly Buchan


3.58

What kind of fated destiny is this
To love and live
To live and love
To live to love
To love to live
Loving so deeply the deepest of oceans didn't compare
But destined to be alone in the end
Falling to the deepest depths
Only to have the slate wiped clean each time
What kind of fated destiny is this
That allows one to become so enraptured with a fellow human
being only to be used for it's own twist of fate
It's own twisted fate
What kind of fated destiny is this
That allows you to fall victim to the hands of the universe
playing carelessly with your heart
Tearing the strings out one by one
Plucking at them like a beautiful harp
What kind of fated destiny is this
That draws in every beautiful thing and chews it up and spits it
out like old stale chewing gum
Removing all of the taste and flavor
Leaving but a wad of sticky tasteless goo
What kind of destiny is this that takes and takes and takes
Like a selfish child constantly demanding more and more to
appease itself
And here you are holding this fated destiny in your hands still
yet with all of it's torn out heart strings
And tears that could have filled the deepest of oceans
Broken dreams of love and living to love and loving to live
Still searching
Looking for that perfect fated destiny
The one with the brand new unchewed gum full of flavor and
taste
For the fated destiny that is full of living to love and loving to
live. Danelle Boyles

3.59
Destiny that trap that bleeds us
Punishes and constrains
As flies in its sticky bonds
We struggle helplessly.  Christine Fowler

3.60
"They may struggle and die but I'll be fine,"
The billionaire says to himself.
"They may struggle and die but I'll be fine,"
As he sits and counts up his wealth.
And we struggled and died
As he went off to hide
But the billionaire slowly died inside
Because all he had left was himself.  Lisa Louise Lovebucket

3.61
Himself and his mind, his senses his thoughts
Reeling in and out over and around , not making much sense or
even in order
Live with them, be with them and sit with them
All he knew was noise and the cacophony was gone, he could
feel all that he was.  Janine Rae

3.62
As the noise of the city, provokes my soul
I yearn for the sounds of birds, wild and free
Where I sit in peace and just be me
Where the leaves dance as the wind blows, where mother
nature feeds my soul
Where songbirds hide in limbs of beautiful trees
Its time to go
I need to be set free.  Leas Cuilinn

3.63
Free to inspire myself,
To walk the time travelled trails of my ancestors,
Or smash the mould to chart innovative paths through
untrodden ways,
Incomprehensibly mine.  Annie Begg

3.64
incomprehensible mine
I take the time
To understand
To realise
That by doing
Nothing,
Doing Nothing

By doing Nothing
I am comprehensively Responsible. Chris Begg

3.65
Responsible me, the one that you see, who follows all rules of
society.
But there's a rebel inside, who is dancing with glee, who digs in
the sand and jumps in the sea.
Who sings along to her own melody and I think I prefer that
irresponsible me!  Sonia Bailey

3.66
An irresponsible melody
the future can but be
to the chords of a present —
the shapes which we hope
will cluster its notes
in a meaning that will outlast
a basso continuo of the past.
Is it a counterpoint?
Is it an intricate planning,
A logic of beauty internal?
Or an afterthought narrative
of cacophony infernal?
And does it matter
how we compose
a music of liquid poetry
or fundamental prose?
A life to interpret like a director a score,
chords and continuo no freedom no more.
But the open white page and unencumbered lines
that long to dream a sound, to sing a heart and give it a body,
free of consequence and free of constraint,
endless possible strokes with which a note to paint,
a somewhere someplace and somebody,
such is the mind that makes and flies
reality and happened fact belies,
as only the future can be
an irresponsible melody. Bert Timmermans

3.67
I love your music and melody, I love your style .
You will always be my celebrity.  Michelle Donna-Marie E
Rivers

3.68
To always be.
To leave a legacy.
A house for the kids and maybe some jewellery.
But would you not prefer to disappear?

Forgotten in eternal rest?
No saddened heir left to shed a tear,
No diamond-studded bequest?
Your name no longer spoken
Your deeds consigned to the past.
"I was not to blame", you could then truthfully claim.
When the planet filled up too fast.  Scott Graham


3.69
When the planet filled up too fast,
There wasn't enough to last,
The rich got greedy,
The poor forever needing.
When the planet filled up too fast,
We had not learned from the past,
We are inadequate.
When the planet filled up too fast,
There was a rise,
The activists tried,
But many lied.
When the planet filled up to fast,
Some tried to make it last,
But others became greedy,
And left the rest of us needy.  Emma Sloan


3.70
Rest is best
With feet up
After a hard day's toil
Be it in the mind or digging in the soil
But.
Above it all
When all is sad and done
Art is often work
But all art should be fun.   Fin Hall


3.71
I always do fun things alone.
I achieve the best result.
I am alone but not lonely.   Sylvia Ang Lay Kheng


3.72
I am alone but not lonely
And seriously, this isn't a
Cliche! There is so much
Work spread on my desk !
If you took me away from it
I would die !
Like fish without water
Like flower away from tree!

But like a lake needs air
River the sea, tree needs sun, we all need each other!
What good is any work
Unappreciated? Unconsumed?
A restaurant cooks to serve
An actor acts to be watched!
Only the birds sing for no one in particular
Not even its mate
Though, if you saw the
Mating dance, you would go
Mad with joy!
In ecstasy of beauty!
A flower blooms for itself
Wilderness is never incomplete!
Nature an endless inspiration
For poets ! Do you detect
A melancholic note?
No my friend! But why isn't
Poetry the life blood of
Human civilisation?
And why are we madly
Fighting a war over oil?
Oh dear! Why did the Gulf war kill so many children ?
And why is there a war
Raging, killing , maiming
In Ukraine? Why are poets
Besieged and beleaguered?
Art centres attacked ?
Civil offices destroyed ?
I am alone but not lonely
But I would be ecstatic
With the triumph of poetry
A celebration outdoors !
With sudden lightening of love, though it deepens only with
time!
But ya, would love to walk
Arm in arm with someone
For years ! N yes, would have loved walking arm in Arm with
someone all these
Years ! But life is full of
Ruptures, myriad twists
That can leave one alone!
I am alone but not lonely
Is not a face saving statement! You can't just
Hold the hands of anyone
And you can't just let
Someone, inside your
Wilderness !
You will agree, right ?     Pankhuri Sinha

3.73
Might is never right.
The powers-that-be
will not agree
But we
who can see
the greed
power breeds
remain powerless, self-righteous
angry but free.
Dare you disagree?   Meher Pestonji

3.72
Dare they disagree?
With him who holds all the cards, the weapons, the money,
The hearts and minds of his people.
You're the David to his Goliath,
Dare you disagree?
Yes, you dared, and more so,
Sing out the Jubilee, fend off the enemy!
Sometimes all it takes is one brave man.   Fiona-Jane Brown

3.73
Or one brave woman or even a cowardly step will do.
Really, it is forward momentum that we are after
Don't get so lost in the problem that you lose sight of the
process.
I wish you all the best and I know – you got this. Special K

3.74
I know, I just know that you will be okay.
You'll cope with all  life throws at you.
You'll follow you're own way.
And so it goes.
The torch is passed to the new generation from the last.  Gaye
Anthony.

3.75
This new generation shall not be the last
Where one is subjugated, victimised
A new gonfalonier will rise, seek justice
Helping all endure life's uncertainties
It is what makes and keeps us human.  Martina McGowan

3.76

Human feelings or extraterrestrial as I am looking into nothing,
But I can see great beauty.
My eyes cannot see but I listen to the quiet. I can hear the
sounds of cosmic beauty but I'm dead how can this be?
I smell something that reminds me of the unseeing - inaudible
natural beauty, oh I wish I was free.
I don't like this feeling of being dead inside, let me pass let my
pain just die.  Dave Bremner

3.77.

Why would I agree to such a passive way of handling pain?
Let it just die???
It never goes away if we just wait...
Easier for a camel to go through the eye of a needle than for me
to agree.  Lia Nogueira

3.78

"It's midnight. Let's leave the arguments and follow the oasis.
How enchanting, what one drink will do.
Turn the saguaro into a camel.
Bring friend back to friend."  Dana Malone

3.79

 Back to the beginning where it all started
The connection, returned, rejoined, renewed
Where stories are told and traded
And memories are shared and cherished
Make me laugh my friend, make me cry
Tell me the truth without fail
But come back to me   Catherine Skalda

3.80

But come back to me
After robbing me blind
You left without one goodbye
You stole my heart
But come back to me
After making love
To revolving door lovers
You fucked me over
But come back to me
After squandering my assets
Now without a pot on piss in
You should have done better
But come back to me
The word again dangled in the distance
tangled in your thoughts
of the last time you visited there
whitewashed almost completely

from your thoughts
until you stumbled past it by chance
standing four square in the woods
in harrowing clarify
just off the main road leading home;
its love like your then partners
swinging in its breeze of a different life
settling its differences in your memories
swapping your misery
for your now happiness.Hunger reduces a man to naught
You eat what you sow
But come back to me
After being cast out
A petty thief deserving nothing
You crawl back begging
But come back to me
After betraying me
I hate myself for welcoming
You home again.
But come back to me
After betraying me
I hate myself for welcoming you home
I say nothing again, but laugh in your face   Kemlyn Tan Bappe

3.81
The word again dangled in the distance
tangled in your thoughts
of the last time you visited there
whitewashed almost completely
from your thoughts
until you stumbled past it by chance
standing four square in the woods
in harrowing clarify
just off the main road leading home;
its love like your then partners
swinging in its breeze of a different life
settling its differences in your memories
swapping your misery
for your now happiness.   Andy N

3.82
For now your  happiness  is the only thing I know
the happiness that I will forever cherish
because of love and fate to bound with you...
Your happiness makes  me feel brand new
your happiness that awakens my heart
that never sees the wonderful smile beyond compare. Mahal
Kuh

3.84
If I have never seen
the wonderful smile
beyond compare
my life would have
been quite different
I might have
amassed riches
and acclamation
but my life would
have been lesser as
I never would have
met and married
Barbara McMullen.  John F McMullen.

3.85
Barbara may be taken but there's someone for us all,
For the longest time I didn't think I could trip and fall,
Thought I was different, thought my heart was cast in stone,
Settled in a house, took a while to find a home,
But now my hat is hung, and I've got some land to roam
Still tearing fences down, building bridges made of stone,
Rising higher still, on solid foundations
Don't have a crown of thorns, but I'm comfy on a throne.
Bruce Alexander Davidson.

3.86

Don't have a crown of thorns

but I'm comfy on a throne.

Anyway, who was ever desirous

of such a mantle of pain?

(Even He died all alone).

Don't possess a retinue of faithful followers

defending my every indiscretion...

Still: who would want for sycophants to smooth their way?

... Open yourself, instead, to even closer inspection.

Don't know of any amount of wealth or fame

that ever did make life that much more grand.

In the-great-scheme-of-things the universe waits patiently:

observes dispassionately... the progress (or otherwise) of Man.

And I don't feel responsible for the hate and the spite

which embroils this lost and forsaken world:

what choices we make, we make as best we can...

and hope in what is subsequently unfurled.　Michael Gerard
Collins

3.87
 Like the thought of a bacon sandwich that will be 'unfurled' on
my plate,
 when you bring the 'bacon' 'back to me' in the hope of feeling
great
Al Buchanan

3.88
I almost turned to vegetarianism, but you saved my bacon.
In life's fried egg disco you cooked breakfasted me, raved with
bacon.
They say it's the hardest thing, the temptation of that smell in
early morning
An integrity testing corridor, that metaphorical path paved with
bacon
So, Dom just nick a blob of brown sauce, a fried egg, melted
cheese,
You can start every new day with a roll, bagel, bap, safe haven
with bacon.  Dominic Williams

3.89
A  roll from the Swedish Smasgoboard would be more filling
for an adventure
 to touch the sky,
before lunch in the clouds.  Kusum Choppra

3.90
Beseech entreat before betray
Fearful tearful distress dismay
Cloudy clouded dismal dreary
Walking wounded heartsick weary
Lunching lurching stagger lumber
Drinking drunken boozy slumber. Lindsey Oliver

3.91
Waking to drunken dreams
Which only put me promptly back under
The spell I have swum in-
From before I knew what it meant…
What it meant… to remember
That I spun in, before I was spent…
That I sang of so gladly in summer.
Words I knew to be so strong…
Despite the way they were were spoken- so tender.
Oh won't you go then!?
Make some sense of it all for me?!
Why do I wake? Why do I drink?
How does it relate to the reason I dream?  Greg Slade

3.92
They say dreams have a reason for appearing at night
They're meant to help you make sense of your plight
Whilst sleeping I danced a jig with a king
Through the blitz of a city, bombs whistling in
The noise was tremendous, the screams, houses hit
The king kept on smiling, he cared not one bit
For the fate of his people, the plain me and you
How to hold any office, he hadn't a clue
The dream's higher purpose I'm led to suspect
Was to let us all know just what's coming next. Keren Hermon

3.93
Next came our unpreparedness;
forewarned, but helpless,
struggling with an unwished for future,
knowing only that we will survive.  Lesley Storm

3.94
Survive to rise into the skies,

Rockets to the moon

Gone too soon

Resume the journey

Retell our story

With roar of power on flames of fury

In glory cross celestial spheres

Chasing echoes of the stars

Mariners seeking Mars

Dream of Dread and Fear

Gods and Titans to hear instead

Tales that banished lord of the dead

 Blazing hope that fades 'gainst heavens trails

Voyagers we seek to know at last

Our future and our past.   Maire Stephens

3.95
Our future goals and our past experiences determine our
present.
Think each goal through according to similar past goals and
successes
and figure out how it may apply to the present: does it
transform
the plans so as to make them unsuitable for execution? Does
any goal
need to be replaced so it doesn't change the path it should take,
or is it the path that needs to be replaced?
We exist in the present because of our past and hope to have a
future based on our thought out goals and plans from our past.
Martina Gallegos

3.96
Let our souls bend like a bow to the constant change a future
brings;
 let us flow as streams, till we join the ocean.  Nabeela Ahmed

3.97
Flow through my ways only to purify my days as time wait for
no man so as death fears no one. Life on earth is like a stream
flowing through the depth of nature, it only ends when another
life begins. Let the ocean waves wash the dirts from the land
and cleanse our souls with pearls deep down in it's bosom
where life dwells. Let us merge together like the stream
flowing to join the ocean for  no man is an island.
Till death do us apart, love still overshadow the hate of the
mind for it's beauty lies in ordinary things mother nature avail
to us. Let thy soul free itself from the misery of mankind, for
life is not predictable on this earth for our bodies are perishable
objects waiting to fade away when the wind blows. Why
destroy when you can build, never rent your life for pleasure
when it doesn't last forever. The hidden truth is mankind most

dangerous enemy for our inactions will not secure our place in the arena of integrity and honesty.
I walk alone now never mean i am alone for the bearer of good news never drown in his own words until the last drop falls. As there is life beneath the ocean so as there is life above it, for nature brings life into reality
Owusu Nyarko Frederick


3.98
Oceans are broad.
Races are liberal.
In oneness we flow as streams to save nature
Moving in diverse course
To converge in an immense expanse
Separating the continents of our differences
Let us flow as streams, till we join the ocean.
Ocean which is water and
Water which is life.
This life is found on land and
Land is nature.
Nature holds us all
So nature breeds life.
The only supreme effort we can make is to reserve it.
You are an ankh and so am I.
Just as droplets of water makes a mighty ocean
We can stretch out this to every drop
As we flow in togetherness so do the beauty of mother nature glow.
Beyond our sights are imaginations of the mind love for unseen barriers of oceans dividing our world into continent's, breathing life into the dead plants for another journey of their life begins. The stream life ends when ocean life begins.
Limits are just smoke screens that you can walk right through .
Free yourself like a stream flow till you join the ocean.
 Osebre Adeline Ann

3.99
Free yourself like a stream, flow till you join the ocean,
it was never this accessible or clear,
hear the sighs of reeds, the near whispers of rain,
let go of pain and memory, swim.
Swim upward, out; then into the open,
gasp and weep when you see the horizon,
flow till you join the ocean, free yourself,
we will be waiting.   Linda Jaxson

3.100

Waiting, on the corner of Dirty Sixth, chestnut brown and
blinding reds.
Watching as Music  seduces Bodies while Drink distracts
Safety at the bar.
I could go to her. They will say carelessness has left her with
broken teeth and torn pants.
My coat whips around my legs and whispers, " don't move,"
"They might say worse of you"
We stand on Dirty Sixth, as silence holds audience and we
wait, fearful of another passive tomorrow.  Dany Morgan


3.101

Fearful of silence ceasing to let go,
it's ghost-ridden embrace forever unravelling
  across the landscape of our futures.    Grace Evans



3.102
                          I
                     was told
                   a decision I
                made could unravel
               my future. But time a.k.a
              past, present, and future is in a
            constant state of flux: present becomes
            past once future happens. This cycle
                    continues
              on a moment-by-moment basis ad
                 infinitum. Think
               of time as a ball of yarn with just
                enough yarn to roll
            down the side of a Giza Pyramid. One
                   end of the
              ball of yarn is attached to a post at the
                     top of
               the pyramid, and, as it rolls down the
                     side of
               the pyramid unraveling, a waggly-
                      tailed
            Labrador retriever impatiently awaits
                its arrival because its owner had
                 soaked a tennis ball in beef
                  broth, let it dry out, then
                 threaded and wrapped
                 enough yarn to roll
                  down the side of
                  a Giza Pyramid,

and, as the ball
of yarn un-
raveled,
the
desert
wind sent
the scent of beef
to the dog, and, when
the tennis ball arrived, the dog
grabbed the ball in its mouth and pulled
it till the final length of yarn exited the
ball.
Think of complete ball of yarn as the
past
which turned into the present as it
unraveled then finally became
the future when the dog
started gnawing at it.
So, if someone
ever tells you a
mistake you
made
could
unravel
your future,
tell them that
the physics of time
disallows for the future
to unravel.
Generalissimo Bryan Ira Franco

MAY  WORDS NEVER FAIL YOU

Printed in Great Britain
by Amazon

82446893R00031